by

Alison McGhee

Pictures by

Harry Bliss

Voyager Books • Harcourt, Inc.
Orlando Austin New York San Diego Toronto London

www.hmhco.com

First Voyager Books edition 2006

Voyager Books is a trademark of Harcourt, Inc.,
registered in the United States of America and/or other jurisdictions.

The Library of Congress has cataloged the hardcover edition as follows:
McGhee, Alison, 1960–
Countdown to kindergarten/Alison McGhee; pictures by Harry Bliss.
p. cm.
Summary: Ten days before the start of kindergarten,
a pre-kindergartner cannot tie her shoes by herself and fears the worst.
[1. Fear—Fiction. 2. Kindergarten—Fiction. 3. First day of school—Fiction. 4. Schools—Fiction.] I. Bliss, Harry, 1964–, ill. II. Title.
PZ7.M4786475Co 2002
[E]—dc21 2001004648
ISBN-13: 978-0152-02516-8 ISBN-10: 0-15-202516-2
ISBN-13: 978-0152-05586-8 pb ISBN-10: 0-15-205586-X pb

SCP 16 15 14 13 12
4500517271

The pictures in this book were done in black ink
and watercolor on Arches 90 lb. watercolor paper.
The display lettering was created by Harry Bliss.
The text type was hand lettered by Paul Colin.
Color separations by Bright Arts Ltd., Hong Kong
Printed in China by RR Donnelley
Production supervision by Ginger Boyer
Designed by Suzanne Fridley

For Devon O'Brien
—A. M.

For Carol Dolnick
—H. B.

I AM IN BIG TROUBLE.

I'm going to kindergarten in ten days. I've heard from a first grader that they have a lot of rules there.

Rule #3: You're not allowed to bring any stuffed animals.

Rule #2: You're not allowed to bring your cat.

Rule #1: You have to know how to tie your shoes. By yourself. You're not allowed to ask for help. Ever.

Want to know what I can do? Count backwards from ten.
SUGAR BLAST
CEREAL
SUGAR BOY
PROOF OF PURCHASE
SUGAR BLAST
CEREAL
WARNING: TOO MUCH OF THIS CEREAL WILL CAUSE TREMORS
KITTY POPS
FREE CAT-NIP
100% WHOLE VERMONT
MILK
FROM THIS COW!

TEN
NINE
EIGHT
SEVEN
SIX
FIVE
FOUR
THREE
TWO
ONE
Want to know what I can't do?

Tie my Shoes.

This isn't getting any easier.

LATER . . .
I know... I'll hide my shoes.
Mom finds everything.
Looky here- the missing shoes and that needle I've been searching for!

Even the rain puddle is out to get me.

I know…I'll pull the laces out. Imagine what could happen if I left them in…

I know…I'll throw them out.

Dad says a lot of five-year-olds don't know how to tie.
I guess he hasn't heard Kindergarten Rule #1.

Dad practices with me.

Look at his knot. Just the way he showed me.

SIX DAYS BEFORE KINDERGARTEN.
50,000 WEEKS ON BEST SELLER LIST
AUTHOR
The Perfect Bow
NEWLY REVISED EDITION
The Perfect Bow
PHOEBE CAULFIELD
What should I try now?
Poor Puddy, you look so hungry.

Puddy, here's your lunch.

LATER THAT DAY...

Mom says a lot of five-year-olds don't know how to tie.
I guess *she* doesn't know about Rule #1, either.

I wonder if you can show up at kindergarten wearing your baby shoes.

Okay. Back to my bedroom for more practice.

Pssst. . . Four Days Before Kindergarten.
How will I ever do it?
What bows!

Poor Mr. Ducky is so sad. He still doesn't know how to tie, either. Maybe a ride in a canoe would cheer him up.
Careful, Mr. Ducky! Don't you know you should never stand up in a canoe?
SHAMPOO
Repeat after me: Shoes are not canoes.

Dad is so nice. He even bought me new laces.
That should help.

LATER THAT DAY...

My parents are taking me out for my favorite dinner—spaghetti—to celebrate the start of school. I don't see anything to celebrate.

Dad says, “Don’t worry, sweetie. It just takes time.” But kindergarten starts in two days! What if I have to wear a sign that says…

ONE DAY BEFORE KINDERGARTEN!

What if they don't let me have playground time and no one gets to see me jump rope counting backwards from ten? What if they don't let me have snack time or I miss the last bell and get locked in school all night without you, Puddy, and I miss my dinner and my dessert and my bedtime story and my good-night kiss? I'm DOOMED!
MEOW (You'll be all right.)

FIRST DAY OF KINDERGARTEN.

LATER THAT MORNING . . .

You only know <u>three</u> kindergartners who can tie their shoes? Three, two, one? That's <u>all</u>?

I thought I was the only one.

I guess I'm not in such big trouble after all.